HIJAB

THE SYMBOL OF MODESTY

AF558888

BABA MAHIR

Copyright © Baba Mahir
All Rights Reserved.

This book has been published with all efforts taken to make the material error-free after the consent of the author. However, the author and the publisher do not assume and hereby disclaim any liability to any party for any loss, damage, or disruption caused by errors or omissions, whether such errors or omissions result from negligence, accident, or any other cause.

While every effort has been made to avoid any mistake or omission, this publication is being sold on the condition and understanding that neither the author nor the publishers or printers would be liable in any manner to any person by reason of any mistake or omission in this publication or for any action taken or omitted to be taken or advice rendered or accepted on the basis of this work. For any defect in printing or binding the publishers will be liable only to replace the defective copy by another copy of this work then available.

TO ALL UMMAH OF PROPHET MUHAMMAD (PBUH)

Contents

Foreword

All Praise be to Allah; we praise and seek Guidance from Him; we have Faith in Him and we place our trust in Him. We seek the Protection of Allah from the evil of our Nafs and our deeds. May He shower Salat and Salam on our beloved Prophet Muhammad () and on his family and his Companions.I have made every attempt to use simple and contemporary English in the translation of this book. However, there were many times where a simple English word could not be found to convey the meaning and, therefore, either the original word in Urdu or Arabic was retained with a footnote explaining its meaning, or a word from old English was substituted.

Preface

In Islam, however, it has a broader meaning. It is the principle of modesty and includes behaviour as well as dress for both males and females. The most visible form of hijab is the head covering that many Muslim women wear. Hijab however goes beyond the head .

In Islamic teachings, it has been said that God has asked women to wear hijab in order to achieve modesty and to redirect the focus of both women and men from the materialistic world towards the more spiritual world of God.

It does not simply stop at covering one's hair. Within the Muslim community, there has been a lot of dispute over whether or not covering the hair is mandatory (fard) to fulfilling the demands of Islam. If this is, in fact, the case, then choosing not to cover one's head would be impermissible (haram) in the faith.

Acknowledgements

First and foremost, I thank Allah (s.w.t.) for His Mercy and Guidance in this work. I also wish to thank Dr. Zubair Mohammad Sofi for Editing this book. He was also kind enough to review the entire book and suggest valuable changes before it was published. I would also like to thank Mr. Shabir Ahmad Lone for their assistance in correcting the translation of various terms and proper nouns. I am thankful as well to Danish Nazir for helping me . Last but not least, I would like to thank my family, especially myfather Nazir Ahmad Lone who have assisted me every step of the way in this work. May Allah be pleased with them.

Baba Mahir

Prologue

There are many issues where there have not been any differences of opinion among the Muslim Ummah since the beginning of Islam. In fact, there has been an almost complete consensus on these issues. But, these are the days of "reform". "Freedom from old traditions" seems to have become the motto. Attempts are being made to approve and accept as lawful everything that was forbidden in Islam. Many consented matters are being presented as controversial. One such issue is that of Hijab . One hears claims from everywhere that there is no Commandment in Islam about Hijab. Some present inaccurate translations of the Holy Verses in this regard. Others bring forth uncommon interpretations of the Qur'anic Verses about Hijab. Still others refute the Ahadith in this respect.In western countries non-Islamic ideologies are more prevalent than Islamic education. The literature about Islam found in these countries has been written mostly by Christians and Jews, or by those so-called Muslims who have been heavily influenced by western education, or have obtained degrees in Islamic Education under the training of Jews and Christians. They, therefore, view the holy Qur'an and Ahadith of the Prophet () through their coloured glasses. As a result, they themselves go astray and lead others on the wrong path as well. Doubts are being created about the Commandments of Hijab also.Hijab, with its established limits, is a Divine Law and Guidance based on the Holy Qur'an and the Traditions (Ahadith) of Prophet Muhammad (), the interpretations of these by the Islamic jurists as well as on the practices of our pious predecessors. It is on these bases that it has been practiced continuously at all times by the Muslim Ummah. It is not something fictitious that was contrived by people and given the status of Islamic Law in Muslim societies based on cultural practices. Such is not the case, nor is it befitting to expect from a comprehensive, complete and protected Divine Constitution of Islam that has no room for any modifications. But, for sometime now, people are going to extremes in its practices and beliefs. Consequently, doubts have been raised in people's minds about the legal status and the basic truth about the Hijab, and it has become the target of questions and doubts.Under the influence of western civilization, the practice of women going about without Hijab has resulted in reactionary and extreme points of views about it. This has caused further doubts about its principles and its legal limits. On the one hand, the legal limits of Hijab are claimed to be the results of conservatism of Islamic scholars and, instead of simply choosing not to observe Hijab for oneself, people are made to believe that bringing women out in the open is the need of the day as well as the objective of the Divine Law. On the other hand, pointing out the legitimate flexibility in the Divine Law about Hijab is considered heresy. This has gone on to the point where the traditional and cultural limits imposed on women are also being incorporated in the Divine Law.It is, therefore, necessary to present the true teachings of the holy Qur'an and the Ahadith on this matter. May Allah give us the true understanding of the Divine Law and the courage to practice it.In the end, I would like to thank my dear sons Mohammed Mansoor and Mohammed Ibrahim, who truly proved to be my hands and arms in writing this book. I am also thankful to my dear friend Maulana Mohammed Abdul Moez who reviewed the transcript and suggested vaulable changes which have made the book better organized and more beneficial. May

Allah () enrich their knowledge and accept them in the service of His Din, and bless them with success of this world and of the world hereafter.NOTE: These days the word Hijab is often translated in English as Head Scarf, which is not in accordance with its meaning and intent in the Holy Qur'an and Ahadith. It is, therefore, misleading. The correct translation is “Something that covers and conceals completely”

ONE

EVIDENCE FROM THE HOLY QUR'AN

The rules and regulations governing the relationship and socialization between men and women are those basics in any human civilization which, when violated, result in the destruction of the entire society. This may be readily witnessed in various times in the history of human civilization. Hence, Allah () has spoken in the Holy Qur'an in detail on this topic providing clear boundaries. For example, men and women have been asked to lower their gazes; women have been asked not to engage in sweet talk with men; and the Companions of the Prophet () were asked to talk to the wives of the Prophet from behind a curtain if they needed to ask anything from them.THE VERSE OF HIJABThe scholars of the Holy Qur'an agree that the command-ment regarding Hijab for women was revealed in the following verse of Surah Ahzab, which is why this verse is also known as the verse of Hijab. 1.) "O you who Believe!

Enter not the Prophet's houses until permission is given to you for a meal, (and then) not (so early as) to wait for its preparation; but when you are invited, enter; and when you have taken your meal, disperse without seeking vain talk. Such (behavior) annoys the Prophet; he is ashamed to dismiss you, but Allah () is not ashamed (to tell you) the truth. And when you ask (his wives) for anything you want, ask them from behind a screen (Hijab); that makes for greater purity for your hearts and for theirs. Nor is it right for you that you should annoy Allah's Messenger, or that you should marry his widows after him at any time. Truly such a thing is in Allah's Sight an enormity." (33:53)In the above verse, we find some etiquettes and command-ments of the Islamic way of life pertaining to:1.Invitations for meals and the conduct of guests.2.Hijab for women, and3.Marriage with the wives of the Prophet () after hisdemise.Since #1 and #3 above are not part of our topic, I will present the details of #2.In this verse of Surah Ahzab, Hijab was mandated for women. Women were not required to observe Hijab before the revelation of this verse.There is consensus among the scholars of the Holy Qur'an that although the wives of the Prophet () were particularly addressed in this verse, the commandment is meant for all women. The same style of providing guidance is found in many other places in the Holy Qur'an. For example, Allah () says in Surah Talaq: (?) "O Prophet (), when you do divorce women, divorce them at their prescribed periods."(65:1)Clearly, not divorcing women in their prescribed periods ('Iddat) and waiting until they are clean, was not meant only for the Prophet () and his wives, but all Muslim men and women are bound by this Divine Law. Similarly, in the above verse of Surah Ahzab, although the address is specific to the wives of the Prophet (), the commandment is meant for all Muslim women. The biggest proof of this is the reason Allah () stated for this command in this verse-"...that makes for greater purity for your hearts and for theirs." This clearly means that immodesty (going without Hijab) breeds filth and indecency in hearts. Undoubtedly, the common Muslim men and women are more in need of protecting themselves from this filth and indecency since they are more liable to engage in such sinful activities.It is also noteworthy here that the women, who have been addressed in this verse of Hijab, were the wives of the Prophet () for whom Allah () Himself took the responsibility to ensure the purity and cleanliness of their hearts. This has been mentioned in the same Surah.) ....(Allah () wishes) to remove all abomination from you and your family members, and to make you pure and spotless. (33:33) On the other hand, the men were those respectable Companions of the Prophet (), many of whom were ahead of the angels in their status. When such pious people of the earlier days of Islam were bound by the commandments of Hijab, the people of later ages would be even more in need of them since the impulsiveness, egocentricity, and sexual freedom will continuously increase as the Day of Judgmentcomes closer. Who among us can claim that our self-control is better than that of the respectable Companions of the Prophet; that our women are more pious than the wives of the Prophet (); and that there is no danger of corruption today in men and women mixing freely with each other.In the interpretation of this verse, Hafiz Ibn Kathir writes:Muslims were forbidden from entering the houses of the Prophet () as they used to enter each other's houses without permission in the days before Islam. Allah () chose modesty and honor for this Ummah and commanded them to observe Hijab. Undoubtedly, this commandment is in respect and honor of this Ummah. (Tafsir Ibn Kathir)'Allamah Ibn 'Arabi writes in his interpretation:Although the three commandments in this verse, i.e., entering the house of the Prophet () after permission, not engaging in idle talk after the meal, and observing Hijab between men and the wives of the Prophet (), were revealed specifically for the houses of the Prophet and his wives, these are binding for all Muslims as we are required to follow the guidance and the tradition of the Prophet (). Unless, of course, if Allah () Himself specifies that a particular rule is meant only for the Prophet () and the Ummah is not subjected to it, which is not the case here. (Ahkam-ul-Qur'an, vol. 5, p. 342) Imam Qurtubi writes:This verse provides the permission to ask, from behind a screen (Hijab), the wives of the Prophet () for any necessary thing, including any matters of religion. And, all Muslim women would be bound by the same rule. Besides this verse, other principles of the Islamic doctrine also tell us that a woman (for her honour) deserves to be hidden - her body as well as her voice. (Tafsir-e-Qurtubi, vol. 14, p. 227)CIRCUMSTANCES SURROUNDING THE REVELATION OF THE ABOVE VERSEA number of circumstances have been stated surrounding the Revelation of the above verse. These are not contradictory. It is likely that all those circumstances together resulted in this Revelation. Ibn Abi Hatim narrated from Salman Bin Arqam (), that the first part of the verse, dealing with the etiquettes of invitations for meal, was revealed about those unruly people who showed up uninvited at meal times and waited until the meal was served.Imam 'Abd Bin Hamid has narrated from Anas () that these people used to wait for the meal time and then went to the house of the Prophet () and sat talking among themselves until the meal was served so that they could join in. The first two verses were revealed to guide such people. These types of incidents occurred before the commandments about Hijab were revealed when men used to go freely into the houses of other people and their private quarters.There are two narrations by Imam Bukhari regarding the circumstances surrounding the Revelation of the commandments about Hijab. One has been narrated by Anas () that 'Umar Bin Khattab () said to the Prophet (): "O Prophet of Allah!, you receive all kinds of people at your home - good and bad; it would be better if you ask your wives to observe Hijab." Accordingly, this verse of Hijab was revealed.There is a narration both in Bukhari and Muslim where 'Umar Faruq () had said: My Lord agreed with me in three things: 1. I said, "O Allah's Apostle! I wish we took the station of Prophet Ibrahim as our praying place (for some of our prayers)"; so came the Divine Inspiration: "And take you (people) the station of Prophet Ibrahim as a place of prayer." (2:125) 2.And as regards the (verse of) the veiling of women, I said, "O Allah's Apostle! I wish you ordered your wives to cover themselves from the men because both the good and bad ones talk to them"; so the verse of Hijab for women was revealed. 3. Once the wives of the Prophet () became envious of each other (for the attention he gave to one of them) and banded together against him, and I said to them, "It may be if he [the Prophet ()] divorced you (all) that his Lord (Allah) will give him, instead of you, wives better than you"; so a verse was revealed in exactly the same words.There is another narration from Anas () in Bukhari: Narrated Anas Bin Malik (): .....I knew about the Order of Al-Hijab (veiling of ladies) more than any other person when it was revealed. It was revealed for the first time when Allah's Apostle () had consummated his marriage with Zainab Bint Jahsh (). When the day dawned, the Prophet was a bridegroom and he invited the people to a banquet; so they came, ate, and then left, all except a few who remained with the Prophet for a long time. The Prophet got up and went out, and I too went out with him so that those people might leave too. The Prophet proceeded and so did I till he came to the threshold of 'Aishah's dwelling place. Then thinking that those people might have left, he returned and so did I along with him and behold, they were still sitting and had not gone. So the Prophet again walked away and I walked along with him. When we reached the threshold of 'Aishah's dwelling place he thought that they had left, and so he returned and I too returned along with him and found those people had left. Then the verse of Hijab was revealed ... (which he recited to me), and drew a curtain between me and him.COMMANDMENT FOR WOMEN TO STAY HOMETo protect the chastity of women and to maintain the moral character of a society, the most important factor is to minimize free contact between men and women. The best way to ensure this is for women not to leave their homes unnecessarily. Their excessive outings and coming in contact with (Ghair-Mahram) men result in severe temptations, which is clearly evident in past and present ignorant societies. This is why the Holy Qur'an specifically commanded women to stay in their homes. Allah () says in Surah Ahzab, verses 32-33:2.-) "O Consorts of the Prophet! You are not like any of the (other) women; if you do fear (Allah), be not too complaisant of speech, lest one in whose heart is a disease should be moved with desire; but speak you a speech (that is) just. And stay quietly in your houses, and make not a dazzling display, like that of the former Times of Ignorance; and establish regular Prayer and give regular charity (Zakat); and obey Allah () and His Messenger. And Allah () only wishes to remove all abomination from you, you Members of the Family, and to make you pure and spotless." (33:32-33)Two important commandments become clear from the above verses.First, that women should not talk to (Ghair-Mahram) men unnecessarily or in a soft and sweet tone of voice, but rather in a straight forward and honorable manner, so that no one will misinterpret them or have any bad thoughts about them.Imam Qurtubi writes in the interpretation of this verse:Allah () has commanded Muslim women to talk in a straight forward and concise manner with (Ghair-Mahram) men. The tone of their voice should be devoid of softness and sweetness unlike the street women and uncivilized women of olden days who used to sweet talk men. A woman should be very careful while talking to (Ghair-Mahram) men even if they are members of her in-laws. She should speak in a firm voice without being loud. (Qurtubi, vol. 14, pp. 177-78)Mufti Muhammad Shafi' writes in his interpretation:means that even when it becomes necessary to talk to the (Ghair-Mahram) men, a woman should avoid the soft and attractive tone of voice which is part of her nature. What this means is that she should not speak in a way that might charm or attract the listener. As Allah () said: "...be not too complaisant of speech, lest one in whose heart is a disease should be moved with desire." Disease here refers to hypocrisy (Nifaq), total or partial. The true hypocrite (Munafiq) would indeed be expected to behave in such a manner, but some times one, who is otherwise a true believer, may also have an inclination towards the forbidden (Haram) which is also part of hypocrisy. A person, who has true Faith, can never be inclined towards the forbidden (Haram).The main objective of this first part of the commandment is for women to acquire such a state of Hijab and an avoidance of (Ghair-Mahram) men that those of weak faith may not have any hope, or greed of any favours, from them. After this verse was revealed, some of the wives of the Prophet () used to cover their mouth with their hands to hide their natural voice while talking to strangers. ‘Amer Bin ‘As narrated from the Prophet ():( )“Indeed the Prophet () prohibited women to talk (to Ghair-Mahram men) without the permission of their husbands.” (Tabrani)The second important part of this commandment states that the best way for women to observe Hijab is to stay in their homes and not to come out without a valid necessity. Observing Hijab in this manner is known as Hijab Bil Buyut (observing Hijab by way of staying home).Also apparent from this verse, is that women are created in a way that they can be contented and at peace only by staying within their houses, occupying themselves with home and family matters. The welfare and prosperity of the society also depends on this. A woman’s physical nature is not well suited for working outside the home like men to earn a living, and to face all the severe hardships associated with it, which only men have been equipped to deal with. This is why, in Islam, women have not been made responsible to earn a living. Her parents and brothers carry the responsibility to meet her material needs before her wedding, which is passed on to her husband after her marriage. This clearly shows how often Islam wants women to come out of their homes.Another part of this verse, "...and make not a dazzling display, like that of the former Times of Ignorance...", tells us that before Islam, women used to roam about without Hijab freely, shamelessly and without any controls. Therefore, the earlier Interpreters of the Holy Qur‘an interpreted these verses in light of the traditions of the former Times of Ignorance. When one reads those interpretations and compares them with the ignorance of the present times, it appears that today people have become even more ignorant than the men in those ancient times.Mujahid and Qatadah say that the word Tabarruj in this versemeans walking in a lewd way. Muqatil states that Tabarruj is when a woman only covers her head with her scarf without covering her neck and chest. Mubarrad says that Tabarruj is when a woman reveals her physical attractiveness which she is required to hide. Lais states that Tabarruj is when a woman does not hide the beauty of her face and her physical shape and considers it good to reveal it. Abu 'Ubaidah () says Tabarruj is when a woman exhibits her beauty and her body in a way as to cause sexual excitement in men. 'Allamah Ibn Jauzi, after quoting the above statements, writes: I believe that coming out of her house and roaming about the streets in itself is sufficient to cause trouble, letalone exhibiting her beauty and her body. (Ahkamun-Nisa') All of the above things, explained by the earlier interpreters under the definition of Tabarruj, are prevalent today. The daughters of the Muslim society today, with a few exceptions, have even gone far beyond. This is despite the fact that the Prophet () has said:() "The worse among the women are those who freely leave their homes without Hijab. They are hypocrites and few of these will enter paradise." (Sunan Al-Baihaqi)It is to dissipate this Tabarruj that the Prophet (), while accepting women in Islam, used to make them promise not to engage in Tabarruj. (Tabrani).From the word Tabarruj in the above verse, it is also clear that if it is necessary for a woman to leave her house, she has to hide her beauty. This can be achieved by wearing a Burqa' or Jalbab that covers her entire body.The advocates of women's freedom often object that the commandments of Hijab in this verse are only meant for the wives of the Prophet (), who are the subjects of this verse, and, therefore, do not apply to all women.In fact, if one reads the complete verse, it is clear that none of the five commandments in this verseare limited only to the wives of the Prophet (). Even the commandments in the verses before and after it are also applicable to all Muslim women. In this verse, the first commandment is about the etiquette of speaking with Ghair-Mahram, then for women to stay in their homes, then to establish the Salat, then to pay the Zakat, and finally to obey Allah () and His Prophet (). Now, who can claim that the commandments related to Salat, Zakat and obedience of Allah () and His Prophet () in this verse are also meant only for the wivesof the Prophet () and that the rest of the women are exempt from these?The truth is that these commandments are meant for all Muslim women, although apparently the first subjects of this verse were the wives of the Prophet (). This has occurred in the Qur'an in many places where the initial address is specific to a person, but the commandment is applicable to all. Imam Abu Bakr Jassas writes in the interpretation of this verse:This verse provides a clear argument that women are required to stay in their homes and it is forbidden for them to leave their homes... And all the etiquettes in this verse were taught to the wives of the Prophet () to safeguard their chastity. All Muslim women are required to follow these commandments. (Jassas, vol. 5, p. 230)'Allamah Ibn Kathir writes:These are the etiquettes Allah () taught the wives of the Prophet () and since all the women of Muslim Ummah are required to follow their example, these commandments are applicable to all Muslim women. (Ibn Kathir, vol. 3, p. 483)Besides, Allah () confirmed the purity and chastity of the wives of the Prophet () in an entire Ruku' of the Qur'an, clearly stating:) Allah () only wishes to remove all abomination from you, you Members of the

Family, and to make you pure and spotless. (33:33)When Allah () Himself confirmed their purity and chastity, can anyone expect them to engage in sweet talk with men while explaining to them matters of religion? When such a thing is not even thinkable, why then did Allah () give them these specific commandments? The answer is that Allah () wanted them to be aware of the natural attraction in a woman's voice and to make a conscious effort to change it with harshness while talking to men so that even this natural delicacy will not become apparent to Ghair-Mahram.The following things are noteworthy here:1.The wives of the Prophet () possess a high status among women. They were cleansed and purified by Allah. No one could even think of them indulging in any sinful activities.2. "They are the Mothers of the Ummah as Allah," proclaimed in Surah Ahzab, verse 6.3.This proclamation was not merely out of respect for them, but as with real mothers, it was forbidden to marry any of them after the demise of the Prophet (). Allah () said:()"....Nor that you should ever marry his widows after him at any time. Indeed that would be an enormity in the sight of Allah." (33:53)

TWO

BURQA' OR JALBAB

In the last verse, Muslim women were asked not to leave their homes without necessity. If they must, they should not go out boldly without Hijab like the women of the olden Days of Ignorance. Further, in Surah Ahzab, Allah () commanded them to use Jalbab when they came out of their homes:3.() “O Prophet! Tell your wives and daughters, and the believing women that they should cast (Yudnina 'Alaihinna) their outer garments (Jalabib) over them; so that it is likelier that they will be known and not harmed; and Allah () is All-Forgiving, Most Merciful.” (33:59)This verse is a very important one among the verses revealed about Hijab, because it clearly states that hiding one's face is included in the commandment of Hijab. Therefore, thescholars and Interpreters of the Holy Qur'an have discussed this issue at great length.Secondly, since this verse is not specifically addressed only to the Consorts of the Prophet (), there is no room to make excuses regarding its applicability to all women.Let us look at the literal meaning of the words Jalbab and Yudnina 'Alaihinna in this verse.WHAT IS

JALBAB?Jalabib is the plural form of the word Jalbab. Many different interpretations have been made in explaining Jalbab. In his research of this word, 'Allamah Ibn Al-Manzur concludes:Jalbab is actually the outer sheet or coverlet which a woman wraps around on top of her garments to cover herself from head to toe. It hides her body completely. (Lisan-ul Arab, vol. 1, p. 273)The root word is Jalbab which is basically used for such things which completely cover something. For example, the blankets we use in cold weather or the darkness of the night which covers all things completely. The word Jalbab is therefore used for that outer sheet which a woman wraps around on top of her clothes to hide herself from the eyes of strangers.In interpreting the word, 'Allamah Ibn Al-Hazam writes:In Arabic language, the language of the Prophet (), Jalbab is that outer sheet which covers the entire body. A piece of cloth which is too small to cover the entire body could not be called Jalbab. (Al-Muhalla, vol. 3, p. 217)In describing it, Ibn Mas'ud () said that Jalbab is that sheet of cloth which is worn on top of the scarf. Ibn 'Abbas () described it as follows:Allah () commanded Muslim women to pull this sheet on top of them to cover their bodies except one eye, when it is necessary for them to come out of their home. (Ibn Kathir)Imam Mohammed Bin Sirin said, "When I asked 'Ubaidah Salmani () the meaning of this verse and how the Jalbab was to be used, he demonstrated it to me by pulling a sheet of cloth over his head to cover his body, leaving his left eye uncovered. This was also the explanation of the word 'Alaihinna in this verse."This verse clearly requires hiding of the face which supports the commandments in the verse of Hijab.The second phrase in this verse which requires interpretation is Yudnina 'Alaihinna. 'Allamah Alusi writes:(The root word) Adna literally means to bring something closer. Here it means to hang something close to you, or over you, since it is followed by 'Ala in the phrase. In my opinion, Adna followed by 'Ala points towards covering themselves with the sheet hanging on top of them in a way so that they can see the road as they walk (Ruh-ul-Ma'ani, vol. 22, pp. 88-89)After quoting and discussing many interpretations, 'Allamah Alusi concludes:All the above discussions deal with explaining the gist (of the term). The apparent meaning of the word 'Alaihinna is clearly to cover one's body completely, although some have interpreted it to mean covering the head and the face, because in the olden Days of Ignorance, women usually left their faces uncovered.HOW TO WRAP THE SHEET AROUNDNot only did the scholars of the Holy Qur'an clarify for us that, according to this verse, it is mandatory for women to wear Hijab and hide their faces, but they also explained exactly how the Jalbab should be worn. The greatest interpreter of the Holy Qur'an, Ibn 'Abbas (), has been reported to have mentioned two ways of wearing Jalbab. The first one, where the sheet of cloth should be pulled over on top to cover the body with the exception of one eye, has been already mentioned above. The second method, which allows for keeping both eyes uncovered, has been reported by 'Allamah Alusi as follows:Ibn Jarir and Ibn Al-Munzir described the method of wearing the Jalbab according to Ibn 'Abbas and Qatadah. The sheet should be wrapped from the top covering the forehead, then bringing one side of the sheet to cover the face below the eyes so that most of the face and the upper body is covered. This will leave both the eyes uncovered (which is acceptable under necessity). (Ruh-ul-Ma'ani, vol. 22, p. 89) Many other scholars, such as Mohammed Bin Sirin, 'Allamah Ibn Jarir, Imam Suddi, Imam Abubakr Jassas, Imam Wahidi, and 'Allamah Ibn Sa'd

Mohammed Bin Ka'b Kurazi, have described the use of Jalbab in more or less the same way as the two ways described by Ibn 'Abbas ().In addition to the scholars mentioned above, all interpreters of the Holy Qur'an, from the time of the Prophet () to the present day, have consistently adhered to the same interpretation of this verse, i.e., women are required to cover them-selves when coming out of their homes and that hiding of the face is included in the Hijab. To quote all these scholars would make this document unnecessarily long, but following are some examples:'Allamah Ibn Jarir writes:In this verse, Allah () is commanding the Prophet () to ask his wives, his daughters and to all Muslim women that they should not dress like slave girls leaving their heads and faces uncovered when they come out of their homes. Instead, they should cover themselves with a cloak covering their faces so that nobody will stand in their way and everyone will know that they are respectable folks. (Tafsir Ibn Jarir, vol. 22, p. 29)'Allamah Nishapuri writes:In the early days of Islam, all women used to come out dressed in knee-length shirts and scarves as was the tradition in the former Days of Ignorance. There was no difference in the dresses of street women and those from respectable families. Then Allah () commanded (Muslim women) to cover their heads and faces so that people would differentiate them from the street women. (Ahkam-ul Qur'an, vol. 4, p. 354) 'Allamah Abu Hayyan states:The advantage in observing Hijab is that these women are recognized as pious and respectable. Thus, the perverts would not be after them and the women would not have to face unpleasantness. Nobody will dare follow and make advances to a woman who has completely concealed herself as opposed to the one who has come out nicely decorated without Hijab; the malicious and evil-minded folks will associate great hopes with such women. (Al-Bahr-ul Muhit, vol. 7, p. 250)These quotations are taken from some of the well-known Interpreters of the Holy Qur'an. Otherwise, almost all the scholars of the Holy Qur'an have been interpreting this verseto include hiding of the face in the commandment of Hijab. It is also noteworthy that among these scholars are the followers of all the four schools of thought. Thus, regardless of whether they are Hanafi, Shaf'i, Humbali or Maliki, all include hiding of the face in the commandmentof Hijab without any disagreement.And, this is not a theoretical matter. We find from the Ahadith and other narrations that all women, including the wives of the Prophet (), immediately implemented this commandment after the Revelation of this verse, and the use of Jalbab and Hijab by women quickly became the norm of the Muslim society. Actually, it was exemplary how readily the Muslim women obeyed and practiced it. Imam Abdul Razzaq narrated from Ummi Salamah (): () After the Revelation of this verse, the ladies of Ansar used to come out of their homes and walk with such dignity as if there were birds sitting on their heads (which would fly away if they walked any faster). And, they used to cover themselves with big black cloaks.It should be noted here that the modern day Burqa' (which is used in some countries by Muslim women) also serves as Jalbab. It is this Hijab, customary among Muslim women since the beginning of Islam, which is now being abolished by those who have been influenced by the western thinking. To accomplish this, they interpret the Holy Qur'an and Ahadith according to their own desires thereby going astray themselves and leading others on the same path. May Allah () guide us and protect us from these mischiefs.THE COMMANDMENT FOR PROTECTING GAZE AND HIDING

ADORNMENTNot only did Islam command women to stay home, to not talk to Ghair-Mahram men seductively, and to cover themselves with cloaks, it barricaded all those roads from where carnal excitement and bad thoughts may attack human beings. Thus, Allah () said (in the Holy Qur'an):4. (-)"Say to the believing men that they should lower their gaze and guard their modesty; that will make for greater purity for them; and Allah () is well acquainted withall that they do. And say to the believing women that they should lower their gaze and guard their modesty; that they should not display their beauty and ornaments except what (must ordinarily) appear thereof; that they should draw their veils over their bosoms and not display their beauty except to their husbands, their fathers, their fathers-in-law, their sons, their step sons, their brothers or their brothers' sons, or their sisters' sons, or their women, or the slaves whom their right hands possess, or male servants free of physical needs, or small children who have no sense of the shame of sex; and that they should not strike their feet in order to draw attention to their hidden ornaments. And O you Believers! Turn you all together towards Allah, that you may attain Bliss." (24:30-31)Before going into the details of the commandments contained in the above two verses, it will be useful to know that the very first verse containing the commandments of Hijab was the one which was mentioned in the beginning of this chapter, i.e., the verse 53 of Surah Ahzab which was revealed at the time of the wedding of Zainab Bint Jahash () to the Prophet (). Scholars have estimated that this verse was revealed in either the 3rd or 5th year of Hijrah. Imam Ibn Kathir and 'Allamah Shaukani believed it to be in the 5th year of Hijra. However, there has been a consensus among all scholars about this verse being the very first one related to the commandments of Hijab. The above two verses of Surah Nur were revealed at the time of the incident of Ifk which occurred upon the return of the Prophet () from the battle of Bani Al-Mustaliq. This battle took place in the 6th year of Hijra, which tells us that these two verses were revealed after the verses of Surah Ahzab. Thus, the commandments of Hijab were implemented when the verses in Surah Ahzab were revealed (which was a year before the above two verses).These verses further contain the following commandments:1. LOWERING THE EYES (GHADD AL-BASAR): The word Yaghuddu in the above verses comes from the root word Ghadd which means to lower, to regulate, to suppress (Mufaradat-ul Qur'an). To lower the eyes in this context means to turn away the eyes from everything forbidden (Tafsir Ibn Kathir). Included in this is looking at a woman with bad intentions and also looking at a woman with no specific intention. As well, it includes looking at those parts of the body of a man or woman which are defined as private (Satr). However, necessities such as medical treatment, are exempt from it. Similarly, to peek into people's houses and to use the eyes in seeing all such things that the religion has forbidden are included under this commandment.2. GUARDING THE MODESTY (PRIVATE PARTS): This implies restraining oneself from all forbidden means to satisfy one's sexual desires. Included in this are adultery, rape, masturbation, homosexuality, lesbianism, etc. With a little analysis, it becomes clear that the intent in these verses is to stop people from all forbidden means of satisfying sexual desires. The beginning and the end points were clearly pointed out (i.e., looking at others with bad intentions and guarding the private parts), and everything in between automatically became part of this commandment. The sexual excitement and mischief indeed begins from freely looking at the opposite sex, and its potential end is indulging in adultery and rape. In between these extremes are sexual fantasies, lewd talk, touching, fondling, etc. 'Allamah Ibn Kathir quotes 'Ubaidah ():()"Everything which is in disobedience of Allah () is a major sin. In this verse, the beginning and the end point of this sin have been identified." (Tafsir Ibn Kathir)3. CONCEALING THE BEAUTY AND ORNAMENTS: What does the word Zinat mean? Maulana Muhammad Idris Kandhalvi writes in the interpretation of this verse:Zinat means beautification, whether it is natural such as face, hands and body, or artificial and intentional such as, clothes, jewelry and make-up. All of these form the apparent beauty of a woman and are included in the meaning of . All of these things, therefore, should be concealed from everyone except the Maharim (those who have been exempted). These have been described in the next verse. The commandments in this verse are mainly related to women's Satr, i.e., an explanation of what parts of a woman's body and her beauty must be concealed from others. In the next verse, exceptions have been listed about the people in front of whom she does not have to observe these restrictions. These are twelve. (Ma'arif-ul Qur'an)Mufti Muhammad Shafi's interpretation of this verse reads: In the beginning of this verse, women were asked not to reveal their beauty. In this part of the verse, they have been asked to conceal their natural beauty as well by covering it with their scarves. The purpose here was also to eradicate the tradition, which was prevalent in the Days of Ignorance, whereby women use to put their scarves on their heads with the sides hanging on the back. This left their ears, neck, collar, and chest exposed. Therefore, Muslim women were asked here not to wear their scarves in this manner, but to wrap the two sides of it closely on top of their chests covering all these parts of the body.Next, those men are described with whom Hijab is not required. There are two reasons for these exceptions.First, there is no danger of any mischief from these men, as they are the Maharim. By nature, these men are the protectors of their women's honour. Second, they live with these women in the same house which also dictates that they be exempted from these restrictions. It is also important to remember that with the exception of the husband, Satr must be observed with the rest of these Maharim men. Exposing of Satr, which is not permissible even in Salat, is forbidden with the Maharim as well.Eight Maharim and four other kinds of men have been exempted in this verse from the commandment of Hijab. Seven of these Maharim were mentioned before in the verseof Hijab in Surah Ahzab. Five other exceptions were mentioned in this verse.It should also be kept in mind that the word Mahram has been used here in its common meaning and includes the husband. The interpretation of Mahram by the scholars, which means "a man with whom marriage is forbidden," is not meant here. Husband: A wife is not required to observe Hijab of any part of her body with her husband. However, to look at the private parts unnecessarily is not preferable. 'Aishah () stated that the Prophet () never looked at her private parts nor did she look at his.Father: The grandfather and the great grand- father are also included in this category.Father-in-Law: The grand father-in-law and the great grandfather-in-law are included here as well.Sons: The real sons.Step-sons.Real and step-brothers. However, cousin brothers, all of whom are considered Ghair-Mahram, are not included in this category.Sons of the real or step brothers.Sons of real and step sisters. Cousin Sisters are not included in here.The above are the eight kinds of Maharim.Women: Hijab does not need to be observed with other Muslim women either, but Satr cannot be exposed to them as well. However, for the purpose of medical treatment, it is permissible. Their women attendants or servants: According to the majority of scholars, male servants are not included in this category. Hijab must be observed with male servants in the same way as with other Ghair-Mahram men. Men who have no interest or desire for women: These are the men who, because of their mental or physical condition, have no interest or desire left in them for the opposite sex.Immature children: Those who have not reached puberty and have not developed an interest or knowledge of the specific matters related to sex and women. Those children who have such knowledge and interest, regardless of their age, will not be included in this category.4. CONCEALING THE SOUND: The fourth important issue that has been discussed in this verse pertains to the sound. Women have been asked not to walk with a heavy foot so as to draw attention of men through the sounds of their jewelry.According to this, to attach any such things to the jewelry which make noise, or to wear jewelry on top of each other producing noise, or to walk in a way so as to create noise of the jewelry which may be heard by Ghair-Mahram men, are all forbidden. From this verse, many jurists have inferred that if it is forbidden to have the Ghair-Mahram men hear the sounds made by pieces of jewelry, it is certainly forbidden for Ghair-Mahram men to hear the voice of women. That is why these jurists have included the voice of a woman in the definition of Satr.Now whether the voice of a woman in itself is a part of her Satr is a controversial issue. Imam Shaf'i has not included it in the definition of Satr for women. There is a difference of opinion among the followers of Imam Abu Hanifah. Ibn

Hammam has included it in Satr which is why it is not preferable for a woman to call Adhan. However, it is evident from Ahadith that the wives of the Prophet () spoke with the Ghair-Mahram men from behind a curtain even after the Revelation of the verse of Hijab. From all of this, it seems that where it has the potential to create Fitnah (mischief) for both the men and women, it is forbidden. Where there is no such likelihood, it is permissible for a woman to speak with a Ghair-Mahram man. To be on the safe side though, it is preferable that women don't talk to Ghair-Mahram men unnecessarily.Imam Jassas, in the interpretation of this verse, wrote:When Allah () has included the sounds of jewelry worn by a woman in the expression of her beauty, it would also be forbidden for a woman to wear colourful and decorated outer garments (like a Jalbab or Burqa', when she is among the Ghair-Mahram men). "And O you Believers, turn you all together towards Allah, so that you may attain Bliss." After commanding men to lower their gaze and women to observe Hijab with Ghair-Mahram men, Allah () instructed all men and women to turn to Him for forgiveness for their shortcomings, and to make a firm determination not to disobey Allah () again. (Ma'arif-ul Qur'an, vol. 6, p. 394)A DANGEROUS MISUNDERSTANDINGIn fact, all the above commands in these verses of Surah Nur are intended to prevent adultery and rape. Thus, these commands provide the best preventative strategies and treatment for the protection of men's and women's honour. Also, these commands are unsurpassable for shaping character and cleansing the inner self (Tazkiyah-i-Batin). However, those whose eyes are blinded with the veil of sexual excitement and hunger are not able to see the beauty of these verses. These lovers of western values and prisoners of their own carnal desires, who wish to do away with these commands of maintaining the honour, try to present the meaning of the phrase, "Except what is apparent outwardly (or what must appear ordinarily)," in this verse in a way that suits their purpose. They claim that since some of the Companions and their followers have been reported to interpret this phrase as meaning the face and hands, it is, therefore, all right for women to roam around publicly with their faces uncovered. This is a misunderstanding which is being promoted for the sheer purpose of following the western values and obtaining freedom from the dictates of the religion.As it has been explained before, the phrase, "Except what is apparent outwardly," is meant to clarify that a woman is allowed to expose her face and hands because some needs and circumstances necessitate it. It does not talk about those needs and circumstances. The next part of this verse, beginning with, "They should draw their veils over their bosoms and not display their beauty except....," describes the limits and boundaries of when and in front of whom may a woman expose her face and hands. It clearly states that women are not to expose their face and hands except in front of Maharim men.Besides, if a woman's face and hands were exempt from the command of concealing her beauty and ornaments, then why was it necessary to list, in the next part of the verse, those people in front of whom she could expose her face and hands? The fact is that the verse, "They should not display their beauty and ornaments except what (must ordinarily) appear thereof," deals with the unexposable parts of a woman's body (Satr) and not with Hijab. The next part of the verse talks about Hijab and the people in front of whom she can come freely with her face and hands exposed, i.e., without Hijab. Thus, the commentators of the Holy Qur'an, such as, Ibn 'Abbas,

Ibn Jarir and Ibn Kathir, have interpreted the verse accordingly. Ibn Kathir, for example,writes:In this verse, Allah () listed the Maharim of a woman and said that although she could expose her beauty in front of these Maharim, but in doing so the intent must not be to show off her adornment. (Tafsir Ibn Kathir, vol. 3, p. 284)Secondly, if women were allowed to go freely with their faces exposed in front of everyone, why was it necessary to command them to guard their eyes (Ghadd Al-Basar) - "And say to the believing women that they should lower their gaze"?Third, if it was permissible for women to go freely in front of anyone with their faces exposed, why did Allah () commanded in Surah Nur to seek permission before entering a household. "O you who believe! Enter not houses other than your own, until you have asked permission....." (24:27)Fourth, Allah () commanded women: "And stay quietly in your houses, and make not a dazzling display, like that of the former Times of Ignorance." If women could go around freely with their faces exposed, why was this command necessary?Fifth, Allah () also commanded: "And when you ask (his wives) for anything you need, ask them from behind a screen; that makes for greater purity for your hearts and for theirs." (Surah Ahzab, v. 53) So, we find out that asking them from behind a screen maintains the purity of hearts and talking to them without any screen may cause contamination of hearts.Sixth, even if a woman needs to talk to a man from behind a screen, she has been commanded to: "Be not too complaisant of speech, lest one in whose heart is a disease should be moved with desire." (Ibid. v. 32) If it was permissible for a woman to go freely in front of men, what was the need for this command?Seventh, Allah () also commanded women: "And that they should not strike their feet in order to draw attention to their hidden ornaments" (Surah Nur, v. 31), because if their attention was drawn to them, it may excite their desires creating the possibility of Fitnah.Now, in the light of all of the above, who, in their right mind, would claim that Islamic Shari'ah which has attempted to close all possible ways to lewdness and sexual excitement and freedom, will permit women to go freely in front of all with their faces exposed, thereby reopening all those paths again?SEEKING PERMISSION BEFORE ENTERING A HOUSEWith respect to Hijab, Islamic Shari'ah also commanded not to enter each other's houses without seeking permission in order to preserve the privacy and sanctity of the household. Allah () says: 5. ( ) "O you who believe! do not enter houses other than your own until you have asked permission and saluted the dwellers therein; that is best for you, (Allah () admonishes you) so that you may heed." (24:27)One of the major reasons for the above commandment is also to ensure that the ladies of the house may move to the inner quarters of the house before a Ghair-Mahram stranger walks in. FOR ELDERLY WOMENFor elderly women, who no longer have sexual desires or the attraction, there is, however, some concession made in these requirements. Allah () says:6.) "O you who believe! Let those whom your right hands possess and the (children) among you who have not come of age ask your permission (before they come to your presence) on three occasions: before the Fajr prayer, the time when you remove your clothes for the noonday heat, and after the Isha prayer; these are your three times of undress; outside those times it is not wrong for you, or for them, to move about attending to each other; thus does Allah () make clear the Signs to you; for Allah () is Full of Knowledge and Wisdom.""But when the children among you come of age let them (also) ask for permission as do those senior to them (in age); thus does Allah () make clear His Signs to you; for Allah () is Full of Knowledge and Wisdom.""Such elderly women as are past the prospect of marriage, there is no blame on them if they lay aside their (outer) garments provided they make not a wilful display of their beauty, but it is best for them to be modest, and Allah () is the One Who sees and knows all things." (24:58-60)The first two verses above allow small children and slaves to move about freely in the house with the exception of thespecified times. Thus, women are also free to be around them without their outer robes.The third verse provides concession for such elderly women who no longer have any desire for marriage or attraction for men, and who can, therefore, take off their outer garments (Burqa', Hijab, robes, etc.) in front of men other than Maharim provided that they do not display their make-up. Although the concession was granted, it was reminded that the preferable thing to do is to be modest.

THREE

EVIDENCE FROM AHADITH

Many Ahadith have already been mentioned in chapter one under the evidence from the Holy Qur'an. The purpose here is not to repeat those Ahadith, but to mention only a few more. To cover all the Ahadith in this regard is neither possible for an incapable person like me nor is it necessary, for I believe that even the evidence from the Holy Qur'an alone is sufficient for one who wishes to follow it; and for those who do not wish to abide by the Divine Law, even the largest collections of the Qur'anic Verses and Ahadith will not suffice. In these modern times, we witness that men and women gather together freely in the name of studying the Holy Qur'an and read these Commandments, but are completely unaffected by them. It is as if they make a mockery of Allah's Commandments by sitting together without any Hijab or partition. For such people, the Prophet () has been reported to have said, "Many who read the Holy Qur'an are such people that the Holy Qur'an itself curses them."First of all, I will mention some Ahadith which show us how the female Companions of the Prophet () vigilantly observed Hijab. There was no difference among them in this regard. They observed Hijab with all men including the Prophet (). They covered their entire bodies including their faces.THE HIJAB OF THE FEMALE COMPANIONS OF THE PROPHETIn a long Hadith, 'Aishah () reports that: 21.() A woman extended her hand from behind a curtain to hand a piece of paper to the Prophet (). The Prophet () pulled his hand back and said, "I don't know if it is a man's or a woman's hand." She said that it was a woman's hand. The Prophet () responded, "If you were a woman, you would have coloured your nails with henna." (Abu Dawud, Nasai)This Hadith is a clear evidence that the female Companions of the Prophet () used to observe Hijab in front of him, which is why the woman extended her hand from behind the curtain. If it was acceptable for women to come without Hijab in front of men, there was no need for it. Besides, if such Hijab was against the Shari'ah of Islam, the Prophet () would have certainly pointed it out to her so that it would not have led others astray.OBSERVANCE OF HIJAB EVEN IN DISTRESS2.() 3Qais Bin Shammas () reported that a female Companion of the Prophet (), whose name was Ummi Khalid, came to see the Prophet () to inquire about her son who had been martyred in a battle. She was hiding her face behind a veil. One of the Companions asked her, "You have come to inquire about your martyred son and you have covered your face with a veil?" She responded, "I am distressed by the loss of my son, I don't wish to be distressed by the loss of my Haya1 as well." The Prophet () said to her, "Your son will have the rewards of two martyrs." She asked him, "How come O Prophet of Allah?" He responded, "Because he was killed by the People of the Book." (Abu Dawud, vol. 1, p. 326) From the above Hadith while it is evident that Ummi Khalid () covered her face in front of the Companions and the Prophet (), we also note how high a standard women had reached in following the Commandments of Hijab. This woman, despite the distress of losing her son, showed high loyalty to the Commands of Allah, and equated the possible distress of losing her Haya to losing her son.We also learn from this Hadith that the Commands of Hijab are essential regardless of the circumstances of sorrow or happiness. Now a days some people believe that under distressing or jubilant circumstances, a person is exempt from following the Divine Law and he/she is not required to follow the Shari'ah. This is clearly a great ignorance. We see women attending funerals and even joining a funeral procession to the graveyard without Hijab, not 1 Modesty, Shyness. As an Islamic term, Hayaimplies modesty and shyness a person feels before his own conscience and before Allah . 4observing Hijab in weddings, and traveling without Hijab. All of these are forbidden.OBSERVING HIJAB WHILE MAKING BAI'AH2The Prophet () himself followed the Commands of Hijab with Ghair-Mahram women. Like men, women also used to make Bai'ah with him. With men, he used to hold their hands in his while making Bai'ah, but with women he made Bai'ah from behind a curtain without holding their hands since holding a Ghair-Mahram woman's hand is as equally forbidden as looking at her.3.( ) Umaimah () reported: I and some other women came to the Prophet () to make Bai'ah on Islam. The women said, "O Prophet of Allah, we make Bai'ah with you on the following conditions - that we will not associate anyone with Allah; that we will not steal; that we will not indulge in fornication and adultery (Zina), that we will not kill our offspring, that we will not wrongfully ascribe our illegitimate children to our husbands; and that we will not disobey you in doing

2 An oath of allegiance to submit and obey. 5good deeds." The Prophet () said to them, "And say that you will follow all these to the best of your ability." The women responded, "Allah and His Prophet are more merciful on us than we are on ourselves; make Bai'ah with us." The Prophet () said to them, "I don't shake hands with women; when I said to you (what I just said), it is as if I had said it to one hundred women." (Mu'atta Imam Malik, Chapter - Bai'ah)With respect to making Bai'ah with women, 'Aishah () provides further clarification.From among women, whoever agreed to these conditions, the Prophet () said to her, "I made Bai'ah with you." By Allah, his hands never touched a woman's hand even at the time of making Bai'ah with them. He used to make Bai'ah with women verbally and then he used to say to them: "I made Bai'ah with you." (Bukhari, the Book of Tafsir)Both of these Ahadith clearly show that the Prophet (), the mentor of all mankind, never touched a woman's hand even at the time of making Bai'ah. When women came to him for this purpose, he made Bai'ah with them verbally. When they insisted upon holding his hand, he told them: "I do not shake hands with women." When Bai'ah may be made verbally with women, why should one hold their hands?OBSERVING HIJAB IN FRONT OF THE COMPANIONS OF THE PROPHETIt is clear from the above Ahadith that the female Companions observed Hijab strictly, even in front of the 6Prophet (). Similarly, the Wives of the Prophet (), although considered as the Mothers of the Ummah, observed strict Hijab in front of all the Companions of the Prophet (). Thus, 'Aishah () states in the detailed Hadith about the incident of Ifk:4.( )I accompanied the Prophet () to the battle of Ifk after the Revelation of the Verses of Hijab..... I arrived back at the army camp after he left with my camel. There was no one left to call or

answer. Everyone had left with the army. I covered myself with my shawl and lied down. A little while later, Safwan Bin Mu'attal passed by me. He was left behind due to some personal reason and had not spent the night with the rest. When he saw me, he came near and recognized me as he had seen me before the Revelation of the Verses of Hijab. He recited loudly, "Inna Lillahi Wa Inna Ilaihi Rajiun.3" His voice woke me up and I covered my face immediately with my shawl. (Muslim, Book of Taubah) 3A verse from the Holy Qur'an meaning: We all belong to Allah and to Him shat we return. This verse is recited upon facing distressful events. 7This Hadith proves in many ways that the Wives of the Prophet () used to observe Hijab.First, the reason why 'Aishah () was left behind in the jungle when the army left, was clearly the fact that their Hijab was not limited to Burqa' or wrapping a shawl around. Instead, they used to travel in a palanquin (Haudaj) mounted on a camel's back. In this incident, when the army was ready to march, the servants carried the Haudaj and mounted it on the camel thinking that 'Aishah () was in it (she had a very slim built in those days), while she had left the Haudaj in the dark to answer the call of nature. Thus, the army left and she was left alone in the jungle. The servants could not look inside the Haudaj to ensure that she was there because it was no longer permissible to do so after the Revelation of the Verses of Hijab.This incident also strongly confirms the fact that women generally used to stay in their homes and used the Haudaj while travelling, which served as an enclosure for them.The statement by 'Aishah () that Safwan Bin Mo'attal recognized her because he had seen her before the Commandments of Hijab, also points to the fact that it was no longer possible for anyone to see the Wives of the Prophet () after these Commands were revealed. She also stated that as soon as she woke up by his voice, she covered her face with her shawl which clearly proves that it was necessary to cover her face as part of Hijab.The fact that the Wives of the Prophet (), in spite of being considered the Mothers of the Ummah, used to observe Hijab is also evident from the incident of Safiyah's () wedding to the Prophet (). Anas () narrates: 8The Prophet stayed for three nights between Khaibar and Madinah and was married to Safiyah. I invited the Muslims to his marriage banquet (Walimah) and there was neither meat nor bread in that banquet but the Prophet ordered Bilal to spread the leather mats on which dates, dried yogurt and butter were put. The Muslims said amongst themselves, "Will she (i.e. Safiyah) be one of the Mothers of the Believers, (i.e. one of the Wives of the Prophet) or just (a lady captive) of what his right-hand possesses." Some of them said, "If the Prophet makes her observe the Hijab, then she will be one of the Mothers of the Believers (i.e. one of the Prophet's Wives), and if he does not make her observe the Hijab, then she will be his lady slave." So when he departed, he made a place for her behind him (on his camel) and made her observe the Hijab. (Bukhari)The above Hadith clearly shows that the Companions of the Prophet () commonly knew that a free woman was required to observe Hijab. Thus, if he asked her to observe Hijab, she would be his wife; otherwise she would be a slave girl. If Hijab had not become customary by then, the Companions would have never thought of this criteria.HIJAB FOR WOMEN SERVANTSAnother thing which should be clearly understood here is that the slave girls or lady captives mentioned in the above Hadith means, women who get captured as prisoners of war in a battle with unbelievers and are distributed among the soldiers to be looked after. These women become legal slave women.

In the present time, there are no such slaves - men or women.The women who are employed to work as household aids do not fall in the category of women slaves. They are required to observe Hijab in the same way as a free woman. 9OBSERVING HIJAB DURING MEDICAL TREATMENTHijab should be observed even during the medical treat-ment as best as possible. Jabir () narrates:5. ()Once Ummi Salamah () asked permission from the Prophet () for Hajamah4. The Prophet () asked Abu Taiba to Cup Ummi Salamah. Jabir () said,"I think the Prophet () asked Abu Taiba to cup Ummi Salamah because either he was her foster brother or a young boy." (Muslim)This Hadith points to the need for Hijab even during medical treatment, because if it was not necessary Jabir () would not have clarified that Abu Taiba was Ummi Salamah's foster brother or a young boy.In this day and age, we see that even in the homes where women observe Hijab, they become quite careless about it when seeking medical treatment. The above Hadith points out that even for medical treatment, one should attempt to go to a Mahram where possible. If one is not available, then a Ghair-Mahram may provide treatment as well. 4 Cupping: The application of a cup shaped instrument to the skin to draw blood for the purpose of bloddletting. 10TO UNCOVER SATR5 FOR MEDICAL TREATMENTIt is permissible to uncover Satr for the purpose of medical treatment, but only as much as absolutely necessary according to this important principle of Shari'ah: . For example, if the doctor can do with checking the pulse and asking for symptoms, he would not be permitted to touch or see any thing else. Similarly, if there is a wound in the arm or ankle, he may see only that part which is affected. If eyes, nose or mouth need to be examined, only those may be uncovered and not the entire face. These restrictions will also be applicable to a doctor who is Mahram for the patient, because even he may not look at the entire body of a Mahram woman. She is not permitted to uncover her back, her front, or her thighs even in front of Maharam. Therefore, if the wound is on one of these body parts, the doctor will be permitted to examine only the place of wound regardless of whether he is a Mahram or not. This may be accomplished by using old clothes with a hole made at the place of wound. Since a woman is not permitted to uncover any parts of her body between the navel and the knees in front of even other women; therefore, even a lady doctor will be permitted to examine these places only as needed through clothes with openings made at the required places. It should also be remembered that while the doctor is examining the patient, the relatives who are present are not permitted to observe those parts; except for such a person who is lawfully permitted to see those body parts. For example, if the doctor is examining the ankle and if the father or a brother is present, they may observe it as it is not unlawful for a Mahram to observe the ankle of a Mahram woman. 5 The whole body of a woman, except her face, hands and feet, is included in the definition of Satr. A woman is not allowed to uncover her Satreven before her father, uncle, brother or son, and during Salah. 11It should be clearly understood that all the above applies to the medical treatment of men as well, as it is not permitted for men to uncover their body parts between the navel and the knee in front of other men. Therefore, if the doctor needs to examine a man's buttocks or give a shot in the behind, he must only see as much of the body part as is absolutely necessary.HIJAB UNDER IHRAMThere is such an emphasis on Hijab in Islamic Shari'ah that even in the state of Ihram, it is necessary to observe Hijab.6.() ‘Aishah () narrated that we were with the Prophet () in the state of Ihram (during Hajj). When men passed by us, we used to pull our shawls down in front of our faces; and when they passed us, we used to lift the shawls up. (Abu Dawud, vol. 1, p. 254)Due to a lack of knowledge, many people believe that Hijab is not necessary in the state of Ihram because it is not permissible to have clothes or anything else touch the face while one is in Ihram. Such beliefs are obviously due to their ignorance as it is clear from the above Hadith that Hijab is necessary even in the state of Ihram. However,there is a slightly different way to observe Hijab during Ihram. For example, wearing a hat with a projected flap around and wearing a veil on top of it in a way that the veil does not touch the face. This is how Hijab is observed by a 12number of women in the state of Ihram. The Wives of the Prophet () also covered their faces with their shawls in front of Ghair-Mahram during Ihram.There is a similar Hadith narrated by Fatimah Bint Mundir. She stated, "In the state of Ihram, we used to cover our faces with our shawls. Asmah (), the daughter of Abubakr Siddiq (), was also with us and she did not stop us from this." (Mu'atta Imam Malik) That is, she did not say to them that it was forbidden to cover their faces during Ihram and that it was not permissible.In another Hadith, ‘Aishah ()narrated that a woman should hang her shawl in front of her face in the state of Ihram (Fath-ul Bari, Book of Hajj).HIJAB WITH IN-LAWSPeople who live in the same household get so close to each other that at times they don’t think about the principles of Shari‘ah. Therefore, Hijab is often not observed with the brothers-in-law; although there is a strong emphasis on observing Hijab with them.7.()‘Uqbah Bin ‘Amir () narrates that the Prophet ()once said, “Do not go near Ghair-Mahram women.” One man asked him, "O Prophet of Allah, what is the Command about the in-laws of a woman?" The Prophet () responded, "The (dangers in not observing Hijab with) in-laws are like death." (Bukhari, Muslim). 13The most noteworthy thing in the above Hadith is the fact that the Prophet () compared the men of in-laws to death. This means that a woman should be even more careful in observing Hijab with her brothers-in-law. Although a woman is required to observe Hijab with all Ghair-Mahram men, to avoid coming in front of the brothers-in-law without Hijab is as important as it is to avoid death.The reason for this is that since these men are considered part of the family, they freely enter the ladies quarters and are frequently even invited in, becoming too close which at times results in illegitimate affairs. The poor husband considers them part of his household and does not even think about stopping them from freely mixing with his wife. But, when they come to his house frequently and if the husband is frequently away, all kinds of seemingly impossible things may occur. It is not as easy for a neighbour to kidnap a woman from his neighbour's house as it is easy for a brother-in-law to kidnap or abuse his sister-in-law.It is because of these reasons that the Prophet () has strongly advised to strictly observe Hijab with the in-laws and to avoide men among the in-laws as one avoids death. Similarly, men of the in-laws have been instructed not to freely mix with their sisters-in-law and not to look at these women.MODESTY (HAYA) AND HONOURAll the Ahadith mentioned above were about observing the Hijab - covering the face and the entire body. The Islamic Shari'ah has not stopped at giving the Commandments of Hijab, it has also clarified every such thing which directly relates to these Commandments and, with the slightest carelessness, may result in vulgarity and shamelessness. In 14other words, many such things have also been forbidden in order to close the doors to indecency and lewdness.Modesty and maintaining one's honour are of primary importance in preserving the moral fibre of any society. This is why modesty has been called the ornament of a woman, which protects her from many sins and which prevents ill-intentioned men from daring to have bad thoughts about her. This modesty has been made part of her nature to safeguard her from being abused by immoral men.8.() 'Abdullah Bin 'Umar () narrated that the Prophet () said, "Indeed Haya (Modesty) and Iman are Companions. When one of them is lifted, the otherleaves as well." (Baihaqi, Shu'abul Iman)In another Hadith, the Prophet () has said that Haya is part of Iman. (Muslim, vol. 1, p. 47)Once the Prophet () saw a man admonishing his brother about Haya. The Prophet said to this man, "Indeed Haya is part of Iman." (Ibid.)In another Hadith, the Prophet () has said, "Only good things result from Haya."In another Hadith he has said, "When lewdness is part of any thing, it becomes defective; and when Haya is part of any thing, it becomes beautiful." (Tirmizi, vol. 2, p. 122) 15In one Hadith, the Prophet () said, "Haya and trustworthiness will be the first things to go from this world; therefore, keep asking Allah for them." (Baihaqi, Firdaus Al-Dailmi)The truth is that Haya is a special characteristic of a Mu'min6. People who are ignorant of the teachings of the Prophet () do not concern themselves with Haya and Honour. Haya and Iman are interdependent; therefore, either they both exist together or they both perish. Thus, the Prophet () has said in one Hadith, "When there is no Haya left in you, then do as you please."Today, vulgarity and all its ingredients have become common place even among well-known Muslims in the zeal of imitating the non-believers. It is these people who have been struggling to bring Muslim women out of Hijab into immodesty and indecency. They have adopted the lifestyle of the Christians more than the traditions of the Prophet (). Such people are in a dilemma. On the one hand, they desire to freely look at the half-clad bodies of the Wives and daughters of other Muslims on the streets; and on the other hand, they do not have the courage to deny the teachings of the Holy Qur'an and Ahadith. Neither can they say that they have given up Islam, nor can they bear to see Muslim women observing Hijab. Actually, indulging in indecency for a long time has killed their sense of honour and modesty which Islam has commanded to preserve. It is this natural desire of maintaining one's honour which compels men to protect the respect and honour of their women. 6 A faithful Muslim who diligently practices faith. 169.()Malik Bin Uhaimir reported that he heard the Prophet () saying that Allah () will not accept any good deeds or worship of an immodest and vulgar person. We asked, "O Prophet of Allah! Who is immodest and vulgar?" He replied, "A man whose wife entertains Ghair-Mahram men." (Kashf-ul Astar 'An Zawaid-ul Barar, p. 187)In another Hadith, the Prophet () has said, "There are three people who will neither go to the Heaven nor will smell even the fragrance of it: first, a man who adopts the appearance of a woman; second, an alcoholic; and third, a Dayyus." People asked, "O Prophet of Allah! Who is a Dayyus?" He replied, "One who tolerates indecency and immorality in his woman." In another narration, his reply has been worded, "One who does not maintain honour and decency in his wife." (Tafsir Ayat-ul Ahkam, vol. 2, p. 167) In yet another narration his reply was: Dayyus is a person who does not care who is visiting his wife. (Tabrani, Jam'ul Fawaid, vol. 1, p. 400)In one Hadith, it has been said that no one has a better sense of honour than Allah which is why he has forbidden lewdness. (Bukhari)Once Sa'd Bin 'Ubadah () said, "I will not hesitate killing my wife with my sword if I see her with a strange 17man." The Prophet () said to the audience, "Are you surprised at Sa'd's sense of honour? I have a higher sense of honour than Sa'd and Allah has it even higher than me."In another Hadith, the Prophet () has said, "I have a sense of honour. Only a person with a darkened heart is deprived of a sense of honour." (Ihya 'Ulum Al-Din) This is to say that a person's exceeding indulgence in indecency results in a loss of wisdom and the ability to differentiate between good and bad.TO GO OUT WITHOUT NECESSITYWith respect to societal purity and Hijab, the Islamic Shari'ah also commands that women should not leave their homes without necessity to reduce the probability of getting into mischief (Fitnah). 10.()Ibn 'Umar () quoted the Prophet () as saying: Women are to be kept in hiding. Indeed when she leaves her home, Shaitan keeps an eye on her. Certainly a woman is closest to Allah when she is in her home. (Tabrani)Truly, a woman is safe from all the mischief until she stays in her home. When she steps out of her home without necessity, she is highly capable of becoming a tool of Shaitan. This is why it has been said in one Hadith that 18when a woman comes in front of a Ghair-Mahram, she comes in the guise of Shaitan. (Abu Dawud, vol. 1, p. 292)In another Hadith, Mu'az () reported the Prophet () as saying: Protect yourselves from the mischief of women, because Iblis7 is a very wise hunter; he hunts very successfully through women. (Firdaus Al-Dailmi, Mirqat, vol. 6, p. 190)In one Hadith, the Prophet () said, "For men, I have not found any mischief (Fitnah) more harmful than women." (Bukhari, Muslim)In another Hadith, he said, "This world is sweet and attractive, and Allah has made you His deputy here. He watches over you to see how you conduct yourselves. You should protect yourself from the love of this world and from the mischief (Fitnah) of women, because the very first mischief in Bani Israil was caused through women."It is a necessary condition for women, in order to preserve their modesty and honour, that they stay in their homes and not step out unnecessarily for fun and to roam around in the market place.Ali () narrates that once the Prophet () asked the Companions, "What is the best thing for a woman?" Nobody answered. Later when I went home, I asked Fatimah the same question. She replied, "The best thing for a woman is to protect herself from the eyes of men." I told the Prophet () Fatimah's answer. He replied, "Indeed, Fatimah is a part of me." (Kashf-ul Astar, p. 150) 7 A name of the Shaitan. 19In another Hadith, the Prophet () has said, "The best deed of the women of my Ummah is contentment and withdrawal from men." (Shara'i Hijab, p. 30)There is so much emphasis placed on women to stay in their homes that their open participation in the important worship like Salat and necessities like funerals and burials is not considered desirable.OFFERING SALAT AT HOMEAs it has been mentioned previously, it is permissible for women to come out of their homes when necessary. And, since Salat is a necessity, it is permissible for them to go to the Masjid (mosque) provided that they cover themselves properly and do not wear perfume and noisy ornaments. In spite of this permission, the Prophet () pronounced that it is better for them to offer their Salat at home.11.()'Abdullah Bin Mas'ud () narrated that the Prophet () said, “It is better for a woman to offer her Salat in her bedroom than in the living room; and it is better for her to offer her Salat in her living room than in her courtyard.” (Abu Dawud, vol. 1, p. 84)In another Hadith, Ummi Salamah () has reported the

Prophet () as saying: the best Masajid (mosques) for women are the innermost rooms of their houses. (Musnad Ahmad) 20In one Hadith, the Prophet () said, "The most likeable Salat of a woman to Allah is the one which she offers in her house privately and in a dark place." (Ibn Khuzaimah)Ibn 'Umar () narrated this saying of the Prophet (): "A woman's Salat which is offered in her privacy is 25 times better than her Salat with congregation." (Kanz Al-Ummal)This has been exaggerated to the point that it was said that for a woman offering her Salat at home is even better than offering in Masjid-al-Haram and Masjid-al-Nabawi where offering one Salat is better than offering 100,000 Salats and 50,000 Salats respectively. Therefore, in Ahadith we find a story of a female Companion of the Prophet (), Ummi Sa'dia (), who came to the Prophet () and said, "O Prophet of Allah! I wish to offer my Salat with you in congregation in the Masjid (mosque)." The Prophet ()replied, "I know how much you desire to offer your Salat behind me in congregation, but offering the Salat in the innermost part of your house is better than offering it in the living room, and offering Salat in the living room is better than offering it in your courtyard, and offering Salat in the courtyard is better than offering it in your neighborhoodMasjid (mosque), and offering your Salat in the neighbor-hood Masjid (mosque) is better than coming to my Masjid (mosque)." (Musnad Ahmad). In Ibn Khuzaimah, this narration also includes the statement that after Ummi Sa'dia heard the Prophet (), she set aside a place in the innermost and darkest corner of her house for Salat and offered her Salat there as long as she lived.'Urwah () narrated this saying of 'Aishah (): The women of Bani Israil used to make wooden sandals which they wore to their places of worship, and they used to 21provide attractions for men; so, Allah forbade them to go to the

Masjid (mosque). (Musnad Abdur Razzaq)In another Hadith, we find this saying of 'Aishah (): If the Prophet () would have seen the attitude of women which they adopted after him, he would have surely stopped them from coming to the Masjid (mosque) as the women of Bani Israil were stopped. (Muslim)PARTICIPATION IN JIHADThe best of the worships is to sacrifice one's life in the path of Allah. However, Islamic Shari'ah has not preferred participation of women even in Jihad, as they may earn the rewards of Jihad without actually participating in it.12.()Anas () reported that once a group of women came to the Prophet () and said, "O Prophet of Allah! Men have reaped all the rewards of participating in Jihad; show us a deed which would help us reach the rewards of the Mujahidin." The Prophet () replied, "Any one of you who stays in her home protecting her modesty and honour will receive the rewards of Jihad." (Musnad Bazzar) 22Once 'Aishah () asked the Prophet (), "O Prophet of Allah! we consider Jihad the best of the deeds; should we not participate in it as well?" He replied, "Women's Jihad is to go for Hajj (Pilgrimage)." (Bukhari)In another Hadith, Abu Qatadah () has reported the Prophet () as saying: Jihad, Friday prayer, and going to the cemetery for burials are not required of women. (Tabrani)ETIQUETTES OF EMERGING FROM HOMEFrom the above Ahadith, it is sufficiently clear that Islamic Shari'ah wants women to emerge from their homes as little as possible. The Shari'ah provides a number of etiquettes for when they need to come out. Among these, Hijab and covering of face have been covered in detail previously.The Use of Perfume and Ornaments: Animportant etiquette is not to come out wearing fragrance and ornaments.13.) Maimunah Bint Sa'd (), who was one of the Prophet's servants, reported him as saying: "A woman who decorates herself for anyone else other than her husband is like such a darkness in the Day of Judgment which has no light in it." (Tirmidhi) 23The women who decorate themselves, freely participate in parties with men, and are considered these days the life of the parties, have been pronounced as the darkness of the parties by the Prophet ().In another Hadith, Maimunah Bint Sa'd narrated that the Prophet () said, "Allah remains displeased with a woman who emerges from her home wearing perfume and gives men the opportunity to look at her, until she returns home." (Tabrani)The Prophet () has also said, "A woman who passes by men wearing perfume so that they will be entertained, is committing adultery; and so are those eyes who look upon her. (Nasai, Ibn Khuzaimah)'Aishah () narrated that once a woman of the Muzainah tribe came to the Prophet () in the Masjid (mosque). She was dressed fashionably and was walking with dalliance. The Prophet () said to the audience, "O people! Stop your women from dressing fashionably and from walking in the Masjid (mosque) with dalliance. Because, Bani Israil were not condemned until their women began to decorate themselves and come to their Masjid (mosque) walking with dalliance." (Ibn Majah)Abu Hurairah () reported that once I saw a woman who was wearing very strong perfume and a tight dress. I asked her: O servant of Allah, are you coming from the Masjid (mosque)? She said: Yes. He said to her: I have heard my beloved Abul Qasim () saying, 'Allah does not accept the Salat of a woman who comes to pray wearing perfume, until she goes home and takes a bath as she does after coition.' (Abu Dawud, vol. 2, p. 219) 24Emerging from Home without Husband's Permission: It is also one of the etiquette for women not to leave their homes without the permission of their husbands.14.()Mu'az () narrates that the Prophet ()

has said, “It is not permissible for any woman who believes in Allah and the Day of Judgment to allow anyone to enter her husband’s house, or to leave home without her husband’s permission; and that she should not obey anyone else in this regard.” (Mustadrak Al-Hakim, Tabrani)The principle of asking the husband’s permission to go out greatly assists a woman to maintain her honour and virtue. Women who go out wherever they want and invite into their homes whomever they want without their husband’s permission, are more likely to lose their honour and character ending up deeper and deeper in a life of sin.Anas () reported the Prophet () as saying: "Any woman who leaves home without her husband’s permission, Allah remains displeased with her until she returns home, or until her husband is pleased with her." (Kanz Al-Ummal)In another Hadith narrated by ‘Umar (), we find that the Prophet () said, "Women should not talk to Ghair-Mahram men without their husband’s permission." (Tabrani) 25Travelling Alone: To protect the honour of women, the Shari‘ah has commanded women to be accompanied by Maharim men when they are travelling, so that they can be protected from mischiefs.15.()‘Abu Sa‘id Khudri () reported that the Prophet ()said, “Any woman who believes in Allah and the Day of Judgement should not travel alone for three days or more except when accompanied by her father, brother, husband, son or any other Mahram man.” (Abu Dawud, Tirmizi, Ibn Majah)The limit of three days, in Shari‘ah, signifies any travel where it becomes permissible to offer Qasr Salat.Ibn ‘Abbas () narrated that the Prophet () said, "No man should be with any woman alone, nor should a woman travel without a Mahram." One man, who heard this, got up and said, "O Prophet of Allah! I have been enlisted in the army to go to such and such battles, but my wife has left for

Hajj." The Prophet () replied, "Go and perform Hajj with your wife." (Bukhari)Walking on the Street: One of the etiquettes for women to emerge from their homes is for them to walk separately from men. The best way to achieve it is to walk on the side of the street. 2616.()Abu Usaid Ansari () reported that once the Prophet () came out of the Masjid (mosque). On the street men and women were walking very close together. When he saw this, he said, "O women! Get in the back. You should walk on the side of the street rather than in the middle." (Abu Dawud, Baihaqi)The narrator reported that afterwards the women became so careful about walking on the sides of the streets that their clothes rubbed against the walls on the sides of the streets.8'Abdullah Bin 'Umar () narrated that the Prophet ()said, "It is not permissible for women to emerge from their homes except in dire necessity; and they should not walk on the street except on the sides." (Tabrani)Anas Bin Malik () narrated that the Prophet () was once going somewhere. In the street, there was a woman walking in front of him. He asked her to walk on a side. She replied, "The road is quite wide." The Companions of the Prophet became quite annoyed. He said to them, "Leave her alone; she is a rebel." (Jami-'ul Usul, vol. 6, p. 660) 8 The streets of Madinah in those days were very narrow with houses on both sides. 27In another Hadith, 'Abdullah Bin 'Umar () narrated that the Prophet () prohibited a man to walk between two women. (Abu Dawud)GUARDING THE EYESTo create a virtuous society and to protect it from sexual anarchy, the Shari'ah, among other things, has commanded to safeguard the eyes. This is because the eyes serve as a messenger. Not guarding the eyes is the first sign of moral decay.17.() 'Abdullah Bin Mas'ud narrated that the Prophet ()said, "The desires and the sins sway the hearts; and Shaitan has high expectations of the eye which is raised to look at a Ghair-Mahram." (Baihaqi)In one Hadith Qudsi, the Prophet () reported that Allah says, "Looking at a Ghair-Mahram is one of the poisoned arrows of Shaitan. Whosoever will stop it (looking at Ghair-Mahram) because of fearing me, I will bless him with such Iman, the sweetness of which he will feel in his heart." (Tabrani, Mustadrak Al-Hakim) This also means that as a punishment of looking at Ghair-Mahram, Allah takes away the sweetness of Iman from a Mu'min.In another Hadith, the Prophet () has said, "On the Day of Judgement, molten lead will be dropped in the eyes of a person who lustfully looks at a woman's beauty." (Az-Zawajir) 28The Prophet () has said in one Hadith, "Lower your gaze and protect your honour; otherwise, your faces will be darkened." (Tabrani)In one Hadith, he said, "Don't sit and wait on the roadside; and if you must, then protect your eyes from looking at the Ghair-Mahram passing by." (Muslim)To safeguard one's eyes and the effort it takes to control one's desires (Nafs) is an on-going good deed which the Prophet () has encouraged in many different ways. For example, he said, "There are three kinds of men whose eyes will not see the hell-fire. One, the eye which is busy watching the enemy during Jihad in the path of Allah; second, the eye which cries with the fear of Allah; and third, the eye which is held from looking at what Allah has forbidden." (Majma'uz-Zawaid)In another Hadith, the Prophet () said, "A Muslim who accidently looks at the beauty of a woman and, instead of continuing to look at her, lowers his gaze will be rewarded by Allah with such worship, the sweetness of which he will clearly feel." (Musnad Ahmad)The Prophet () has also said, "If you guarantee me six things, I will guarantee Paradise for you: 1) When you speak, do not lie; 2) Do not breach your trust;

3) Do not break a promise; 4) Lower your gaze; 5) Protect your hands from oppression; and 6) Guard your honour." (Musnad Ahmad, vol. 5, p. 323)In one Hadith, the Prophet () said, "Be very clear that Allah curses the person who looks at Ghair-Mahram and exhibits himself/herself in front of them." (Mishkat, p. 270) 29This Hadith provides a lot of other details. In principle, it denounces all forbidden gazes. It not only condemns the person who is gazing but also the one who is willfully showing off himself or herself. A person who opens any such part of his/her body, which is not permissible to look at by others, and the one who looks at it, both deserve to be cursed.Willfully Going to a Place Where Hijab is not being Observed: In the interpretation of the above Hadith, the following circumstances are also included where men and women would deserve to be cursed by Allah. Any woman who goes out to the market place or any other public place without Hijab and the Ghair-Mahram men who gaze at her.A woman who stands in her balcony, window or sun deck without Hijab where she can see and be seen by Ghair-Mahram men.In weddings, the bridegroom who goes in the ladies section, where he can see and be seen by Ghair-Mahram women.A woman who uncovers any part of her body between the navel and just below the knees in front of another woman. Similarly, a man who uncovers these parts of his body in front of another man.A woman who uncovers any part of her body in front of her Maharam, such as her father, brother, etc. Today in many westernized homes, women, following the footsteps of their western sisters, wear short dresses with underwears which leave their thighs and legs visible to all men in the home including the male servants (who, by the way, should not 30be allowed to come in the ladies quarters). Thus, all men and women of the household

become deserving of the curse by Allah. Lastly, it should be understood about Ghadd Al-Basar (guarding the eyes) that it is not permissible to intentionally look at Ghair-Mahram, but if one unintentionally looked at one, he/she should not continue to stare or to have a second look. Thus, we find in a Hadith narrated by Jarir Bin 'Abdullah Bajali () that he asked the Prophet () about the sudden and unintentional glimpse (at a Ghair-Mahram). He replied, "Turn your eyes away." (Muslim, Tirmizi) In another Hadith, the Prophet () said to Ali (), "O Ali! You have a large share in the Paradise. Do not look at a Ghair-Mahram again after the first unintentional look. The unintentional look is forgiven." (Musnad Bazzar)BEING ALONE WITH GHAIR-MAHRAM MANWhen a Ghair-Mahram man and woman live together or meet in privacy, it often results in illegitimate and immoral conduct. This is why the Shari'ah has forbidden it to prevent corruption.18.() 'Umar () narrated that the Prophet () said, "When a Ghair-Mahram man and woman meet in privacy, the third one present is Shaitan." (Tirmizi)We know that Shaitan's job is to lead people astray. When a man and woman are meeting together in privacy, he is there to emotionally excite them and to invite them to 31engage in unbecoming conduct. This is why the Prophet () has prohibited it. It is necessary to emphatically follow this prohibition. Even elders, teachers, mentors, and cousins should strongly avoid being with Ghair-Mahram in privacy. Doing so is sinful.'Amr Bin Al-'As () narrated that the Prophet ()prohibited them to visit women without their husband's permission.9In another Hadith, the Prophet () said, "Do not visit women in the absence of their husbands because Shaitan circulates inside you like your blood." (Tirmizi)In one Hadith, the Prophet () said, "After today, nobody should visit any woman in the absence of her husband unless he is accompanied by a few other men."The Prophet () has also said, "Do not visit the Wives of Mujahidin while they are away from their homes." (Kashf-ul Astar, p. 216)Jabir () narrated a Hadith where the Prophet () said, "Beware, no one should spend a night alone in a house with a single (divorced or widowed) woman unless he is married to her, or happens to be her Mahram." (Muslim)In the above Hadith, it is prohibited for any man to spend a night alone in a house with a Ghair-Mahram woman. This prohibition is based on foresight and wisdom. In principle, it is prohibited for a Ghair-Mahram man and woman to be alone together under all circumstances, but the specific 9This and the following two Ahadith pertain to the circumstances that necessitate Ghair-Mahram men visiting women. Under all such circumstances, Hijabmust be observed. 32prohibition of spending a night alone under one roof has been separately mentioned, because in the darkness of night where others are not likely to witness any thing, the opportunities for misconduct are greater. Again, all the Ghair-Mahram relatives, such as cousins and brothers-inlaw, are also included in this prohibition. Often, women do not take precaution with these men and go in front of them without Hijab unhesitantly. This prohibition is both for men and women. Men have been addressed in the Hadith, because they are stronger and may not be easily deterred bya woman.'Allamah Nawawi writes in the Sharah Muslim that the reason why divorced and widowed women were separately mentioned in this Hadith is that due to being alone, these women become easy prey for men who are looking to marry or have bad intentions otherwise. They will not dare to visit single girls because they protect themselves and are also protected by their parents.

The Ancient Age Ofjahiliyah And Present Day Jahiliyah

Thousands of years ago, two ages passed to which the Holy Qur'an has referred as the initial Ages of Jahiliyah: one is the age between the coming of the Prophets Nuh and Idris () and the other between the time of Isa () and our Prophet (). The women of these ages exposed their bodies and abused their freedom to leave their homes to an extent unheard of before that time. As a result they came to be regarded as objects to be exhibited and taken advantage of by all. They were no longer like precious treasures to be protected by those whom they rightfully belonged to, but had become like public charity which could be utilized by anybody at any time. They walked the streets, well-decorated with jewelry and perfumes, attracting men with their flirtatious mannerism as well as by showing off their beauty and half-clad bodies. The frequent contact of women with men other than their husbands created a situation whereby it was possible for a woman to be used by her husband and a lover at the same time. Not having any regard for their honour, respect, chastity and modesty, these women had no hesitation to please men with anything they could ever want from a woman. It was these shameless behaviours and immoral acts of those olden days which the Holy Qur'an referred to as Tabarruj Al-Jahiliyah.Today's licentious societies, and in particular, the West's pleasure-loving but cultured communities, have gone so far in their lewdness and indecencies that they have managed to put even the past Ages of Jahiliyah

9 798887 496924

Printed by Libri Plureos GmbH in Hamburg,
Germany